Rise
Recreation

Women's Voices, Women's Lives
Celebrating International Women's Day

BLUE FORGE PRESS
Port Orchard, Washington

Rise: Recreation
Women's Voices, Women's Lives
Copyright 2024 by Blue Forge Press

First eBook Edition March 2024
First Print Edition March 2024

Cover design by Brianne DiMarco
Interior design by Brianne DiMarco

ISBN 978-1-59092-998-8

For information about film, reprint or other subsidiary rights, contact blueforgegroup@gmail.com

Blue Forge Press is the print division of the volunteer-run, federal 501 (c)3 nonprofit company, Blue Forge Group, founded in 1989 and dedicated to bringing light to the shadows and voice to the silence. We strive to empower storytellers across all walks of life with our four divisions: Blue Forge Press, Blue Forge Films, Blue Forge Gaming, and Blue Forge Records. Find out more at www.BlueForgeGroup.org

Blue Forge Press
7419 Ebbert Drive Southeast
Port Orchard, Washington 98367
blueforgepress@gmail.com
360-550-2071 ph.txt

*For the artists, the athletes,
the adventurers, and the amazons*

Table of Contents

Recreation

POETRY

Michelle Lee

Somebody

I used to be somebody:

    seeking ways to grow, learn,

    sprout new starts,

        like a spring morning rebirth;

    taking life's lessons

    and planting seeds

        to nurture,

        shape,

        encourage

    to be strong and provide.

I used to be somebody:

    warm as a summer night.

    Filled with love and promise,

    my heart a bounty

    to be shared with all;

        plenty to give,

        thriving,

        happy,

        eager,

    ready for adventure.

I used to be somebody:

    fierce, proud, admired,

    and ignored all the warnings

the crisp fall heralded in.
The deceptively beautiful skies
with the cold wind
that shredded your soul,
signaling change;
     farewells,
     loss disguised as
     unimaginable beauty,
     magic
     turned dark,
     vivid colors
     muted by morning fog.
Drifting,
free falling,
floating.
I used to be somebody:
     loved, important, wanted,
     now I'm an isolated mountaintop,
     a frozen, lonely peak
     in the middle of winter;
     insurmountable,
     unattainable,
     dangerous,
     full of crevasses, fractures,
     forgotten.

I'd gotten used to being somebody,
until the change of seasons
reminded me of the cycle:
birth to death,
somebody to nobody,
and the embers
became ashes,
in the frigid darkness
of the night.

Fine

Because if I admit that I'm not,

    that's when the anchor sinks me,

    pulls me down to the depths

    that I can't survive in;

        deprives me of oxygen,

        and light.

Unfortunately, my brain thinks

    the chain holding that anchor

        is a lifeline,

        a safety.

    And I don't realize,

    or understand,

    and don't know how,

        to let go.

    Allow myself

        to swim,

        to surface,

        to breathe,

    to flounder like so many others

    while they wait for help;

        or strength,

to prove it's in our own power

    to overcome.

    To prevail,

    or to reach out

to those watching in silent agony,

because they want me to grab

    the outstretched hand.

Willingly offered.

All I know is the lie

that I tell myself,

and try to make others believe:

    I'm fine.

Wisdom

The old lady's head shook as she said,

"It just don't feel right."

She pushed the money back.

The weathered face

with deep lines etched into the frail skin

slowly spread into a toothy smile

that was more gaps than teeth.

The corners of her eyes wrinkled even more

and hooded the orbs that had more depth

than the unexplored trenches in the ocean.

"I, too, know what it means to suffer," she said.

"I was reborn to be me."

And she lovingly held out the loaf of bread

with hands that were laden with swollen knuckles,

her fingers so bent, twisted, and gnarled

that it reminded the young girl

of the old trees that withstood time and wars.

The old lady's hands shook

as if the bread were the heaviest thing

that she'd had to lift the whole day;

yet the paper-thin, scarred skin

with rivers of veins that wound down her arms

told a different story than her smile.

It spoke of miles of loss.

The girl took the bread,

too hungry to go without again and pocketed her money.

She didn't have the wisdom to understand

the suffering the woman spoke of;

she didn't possess the knowledge

of the cruelty dealt at the hands of others.

But the girl still grasped the woman's hand,

brought it to her cheek,

and held it there in gratitude

that she wouldn't be hungry that night.

Only then did she see the distorted

tattooed number

hidden under the tattered sleeve;

which didn't make much sense to her young mind.

It would only be years later

that she began to understand

the strength of character it took

to be kind;

when the world tried to kill you,

for simply existing;

that love

could come from a loaf of bread.

Hate

I should hate you.
I wanted to, even tried to
for the brutal way
you sliced me down,
left everything unsaid,
and denied me closure.

Instead, I hated me
for a host of reasons.
None of which
were previously on my radar
of insecurities and imperfections.

I didn't hate the darkness
that drowned me,
but I didn't want to be stuck
choking on anger,
regret,
despair.
For the moment, though,
it was comfort.

I needed to hate you
to give me momentum,
to find me;
the one buried
under the litany of excuses
you used to condemn me,
and crucify me.
The hate would be my fuel
to keep me moving,
but it wasn't there.

I found apathy in its place,
at least, where you were concerned.
I learned to face the mirror
and see myself
through eyes other than yours.
Despite it all,
beneath the apathy,
I once loved you.
And that won't die,
even if
I should hate you.

Fall

The first change was subtle;
     but the signs were evident.
The spirits dancing across
     my exposed flesh with the breeze
      was raising my hair,
     colors flitted through my vision.
A warning of the slow
     yet beautiful death to come.
The glacier blue churning water
     of the icy river
battled the heat of the day,
     and the battered yellow leaf
fought against drowning
     as it tried to float to freedom,
tugging on my heartstrings
     and taking my bruised heart
      along for the turbulent ride.
Melancholy settled on my soul,
     a gentle weight reminding me
      the cycle of life continues
     and there is beauty in endings.

Mother nature had an uncanny way
          of reflecting
that which we harbor inside,
          then showing us
where the beauty hides
          to soothe the ache.
The first change was subtle,
          but fall in her stunning glory,
will usher in the new season
                    mirroring life after loss.

I Need

I need to shatter
and lose some pieces;
the parts that no longer fit,
or provide sustenance to my life.

I need to break
the perceived rusted-out chains
of oppression
I used to bind myself.

I need to change,
like the wild and untamed Mother Nature,
and adapt to hostilities
self-imposed.

I need to crumble
under the immense weight
of my expectations,
so that I learn self-care.

I need to recreate,
reestablish, reinforce,

the lacking parts of my soul
I neglected.

I need to learn:
new patterns, behaviors,
and admit I'm human;
I'm only one person, I can't fix everything.

I need to understand
that I matter;
to myself and those around me,
to use my voice not only for others.

I need to rest
my aching body, my exhausted soul,
my ever-racing, nonstop mind;
stop being my own enemy.

I need to believe:
I am enough;
for you, for whatever comes my way;
for myself.

Dakoda Foxx

My Breath

I can hardly catch my breath
in a gleam of your dew
it fell on me
like morning rain.

To see the mist of your haze
I orbit past your space, Orion
and have nothing on you
in the morning dew.

And that is when
I think of you.

Even When

Even when my love seems to fall
my love is always with thee.
Even when the moon goes and hides
you're the only sun I see.

When you think I have fallen down
I will swim to you though the seas.
Even when you can feel my love
look up, look for the moon
and you will see me.

I am like the moon, my love.
I am never unseen.
I am everywhere you go,
day or night you can find me.

That's when you know that love is real
'cause you can feel me
even when the lights go out .

Look up, you will see me.

We will join together, my love
when the moon and the sun meet.

Even when my love seems to fall
my love is always with thee.
Even when the moon goes and hides
you're the only sun I see.

I am your moon and your my sun.
Even when you think I'm gone
I am always with thee.

Dear Future Wife,

I pray that you find me well.
I pray that you love Halloween
    just as much as I do.
I pray you are kind, sweet,
    and funny.
I pray you love to be touched
    as I love to touch you.
I pray you love to touch me
    as I love to be touched.
I pray that you like to talk
    as I love to be talked to.
I pray you like to cuddle
    for I love to cuddle.
I pray that you can hear my heart
    for it's always speaking to you.

Look to the Future

Looking ahead to search for the thing
    that will bring me peace.
Hope and joy is the best outcome
    for a new start.
Looking forward to what the year
    has in store for me.
April showers bring me
    tons of flowers.
Looking forward to hearing the music
    that makes me move.
Enjoying life as it comes, looking forward
    to brighter day's adventures.
Looking for the best outcome
    for me.
Looking for the best adventures
    that await me.

Moving

So many times on our journeys
we lose sight of our goals
on the path.
If we keep our eyes
on what is ahead
we won't veer off the path.
If we're at a stand still
on what to do
move forward and then
you will see that
your goal is in your reach.

Jennifer DiMarco

At Sea

The ocean has been
green, teal, denim, dark blue,
black, froth-white, and now:
steel grey
gunmetal grey
unpolished pewter
silver left to tarnish
with the rough passage of time
as we travel down
the Inside Passage.

Eight days
one hundred eighty-four hours
on this wide water
this vast vista
of unbroken sea and sky
yet still
(always and forever)
she is as unpredictable
as mysterious
as unknowable
as powerful
as you are.

For five thousand five hundred years

men have sailed the sea

yet still

    (always and forever)

she remains her only keeper.

Did I think a woman

would know her better

the way it took a woman

to mend your heart?

You are reflected in the glass

floor to ceiling

four inches thick

peppered with swollen drops

that pop and patter

a multidirectional, antigravity dance

as the winds best eighty

and the waves break at sixteen,

eighteen

twenty.

The ice shed shatters

    (canvas white and tanzanite

    each the size of our home

    two thousand nautical miles away)

across the steel bow
a towering, arching sentinel without
a figure head?
Mast head?
Maiden head?
I am a creature of soil and stone
of prose and numbers
angles and wood.
I don't have these answers.

It is you who swims
in lakes, rivers and seas.
It was your ancestors who sailed
and saw and settled.
It is you who knows these things
        (and so many others)
that we need to navigate
to dive deep into this world
not quite our own.

A dense, heavy mist
opaque as Carrara marble
        (Luna marble
        to my Roman ancestors)
takes the view

erasing it from existence
as we sit
not touching
and watch the ocean
instead of each other.

A low, slow, drawn-out moan:
The fog horn through the erasure
warns and shares our wariness.
We are safe and unsafe
in equal measure.
We keep a distance
        (so publicly acceptable)
between us to survive
but my desire
has nothing to do
with politics and policing
and everything to do with
your hands
your hips
the shape of your lips
the joy in your eyes
the rise and fall of
your chest where I wish
to rest my head.

This journey
is eight days
and our journey
is decades more
and a decade prior.
Every
single
day
I discover
something
anything
everything
new about you.

This old dog
        (like my first dog)
knows no tricks
but I grow ever more loyal
with every sunrise
and every sunset
each and every
rewind and reset.

I dreamt last night
of spider rain
and woke myself like a child
weeping, "Spiders... spiders...."

"I'll get them," you assure me
still sound asleep.
"They won't hurt you."
And you draw me into your arms
my head to your heart
my body tucked
          (an impossibly perfect fit)
like two puzzle pieces
completing one picture
in the quiet dark of our cabin
the size of an ample cubby.
It's hard to remain afraid
when you are so sure.

I understand religion
for the first time.

On the small table
between our wicker deck chairs
our drinks sway lazily
in their tall, frosted glasses.
          (They exist
          under their own influence
          apparently unaffected
          by the oscillations
          of the ocean.)

Cucumber, mint, jalapeño and lime.
This white rum is nothing like
the sharp tequila, bright vodka, smooth THC
we share at home.
The ice cubes
        (assuming spherical)
are arctic marbles
denting one another
with small, soft sounds
like wrens across new snow.

I so desperately
don't want to be here
at sea
adrift
apathetic
to myself.

At almost-fifty
I am already
the stump
of the Giving Tree.
"Sit and rest," I tell you.
But you will not burden me.
Instead you
        (my selkie turned garden witch)

coax me with warm rain
and warmer sunshine
to sprout anew.

You are trying to teach me
to re-teach me
in a way that
allows me to rewild.
I am the Red Fox
to your Little Prince
pleading for you
to mark me
inerasable, ineradicable
with my love for you.
So why do I shrink away
hiss and strike
like Kipling's Kaa?
If you tame me?
I strike!
If you don't?
I strike!

Yet still
over and again
    (always and forever)

you throw wide
your arms
your heart
and insist:

"How can you think I don't want you? How can you think I only love you platonically? I know my own thoughts and my own feelings. I'm incredibly physically attracted to you and I have been since before we started dating. I find it difficult to take my eyes off you when you're in the room with me—even thirteen years later. I often stare at your ass (just being honest). I try not to leer at you when you're undressing because I don't want to scare you away, but I find your naked body deeply beautiful. Your thighs drive me wild. When I see them, I want to touch you. I want to pull you into my arms and make love. Touching you turns me on in a way that nothing else does. I know it's been a long time since you felt safe enough in your own skin to let me, but those moments are indelible in my memory, written into my lifeline. The passion I feel for you leaves me breathless."

How am I to argue?
How can I deny you?
And yet... and yet....

Here we are at sea.
My beloved and me.

As I stare into corners and
walk out of elevators
on the wrong floor and
cry soundlessly
in public bathroom stalls.

Here we are.

Beaten down but rising
cresting to crash.
And while I would rather be
almost anywhere
but here
I want to be
with no one else
but you.

Bree Indigo

Signs of Spring

winter weighs heavy
shadows stretch long
and the chill settles
deep in my marrow
naked branches reach
toward a fleeting gunmetal sky
and even the evergreens seem
to hold their breath

on the lingering dusk
of winter's shadow
it seems
the darkness and cold
might never retreat

but in the liminal silence
a heartbeat pulses
barely perceptible at first
buds and leaves emerge
through frost and ice
roots sipping melting snow
as sunlight warms the soil

a symphony of life
beneath the thawing earth
the first notes hesitant
but a necessary reminder

sure as dawn dispels night
the light will return
finally the cold will yield
and I'll find my smile
once again

Rainfall

water steams

collecting in beads

at the cut end of the firewood

until gravity weighs too heavy

each drop falling

in its own time

hissing and crackling

as it meets

glowing embers

I am grateful for the timber

the heat it provides

a warm embrace against

the cold, damp, wet

of our Pacific Northwest winter

but the madrona was old

older than me and our house

    (both est. 1988)

and I stopped counting the rings

when I realized how many decades

this sentinel stood

protecting the land

that is not really ours
and I wished for a moment
(unreasonably)
we had let the tree stay
and grow precariously
threatening the neighbor's property
if she happened to
(decided to?)
fall

did her roots drink deeply
that first night
you stood in the rain
at our wrought iron gate?
the night before the afternoon
I kissed you on our porch
for better or worse
our whole lives entwined
from that moment on

I reach out
fearless in that moment
somehow still the child I was
(and the woman I am)
pokey and wild and

unafraid to be burned
and touch the droplet
the memories warm and slick
on my fingertips
I think of every rainfall
between that first one
and the most recent
(though certainly not the last)
and ponder
how many memories
one tree can hold

a four foot stump remains
but the sentinel still grows
new branches reaching
toward sky and sun
both a shadow of what was
and a promise of what can be

Cloch na Blarnan

deep, dark emerald green
a glance in a cafe
(is it still window shopping
if I'm inside the shop?)
and I'm brought back
two decades
in an instant

you were so ecstatic
about your new SUV
well-deserved after years
of minivans and carpools
finally something just for you

your favorite color
deep, dark emerald green
so dark it seems nearly black
metallic paint glitter in the sun
in front of your house
with the claddagh address plaque
above the lake

we drive past that house
every christmas
my children enjoying
the neighborhood light displays
while I remember you
the holidays and good times

before grandpa left you
before the day
we thought you might not survive
and I visited my grandmother
in the E.R. psych ward
after junior high track practice
before our family imploded
an indefinite, irreparable
shattered looking glass

I try to recreate what is
and what was
holding on to the good
reframing the bad
recycle, reuse
shards of mosaic glass
under my feet in the garden

the moss growing thicker
each year
until one day
the stepping stones
disappear altogether
and only your ghosts
remain

The Infinite Grey

the fog erases
what we know
should be

trees disappear and
roads cut through
endless grey clouds
giving way to
veins of ochre
leaves dead
and discarded

but we trust that
we know what resides
outside the fog

we trust that
the topography
we've memorized
inch by inch
a fingerprint at a time
will still be

the azure tides and
bronze-tinged forests
we know

an earthquake—
techtonic plates shift
tension breaking
along fault lines
rupturing, exploding
steam escaping
in muffled gasps

sunlight breaks
through the infinite grey
fog dissipating
like it never existed
and the ocean pulls
toward the horizon
so far away
I wonder if
she'll ever return

sand stretches
toward sky
a sudden and uninvited
desert

but the horizon rises

impossibly tall

towering

until it crashes over us

in waves of blue

—a tidal wave

Jonielle McMurtrey

Rebirth

Today
Seven years ago
You tried to take my life
For the last time

The first time
My birthday in 2013/14
That one is fuzzy
The second time
Easter 2016
The last time
4/29/2016
Those things you did to me
They are no longer a part of me

Seven years they say
It takes a body
To replace
Every part of itself

The part you squeezed
Trying to cut my air off
Is free from you forever

The part you held down
As you took what you wanted
Has been touched by loving hands
And will never remember
What you took from it
Without permission
The part you slammed
Against the shower wall
And on the floor
Has been reborn
And will never know
That pain again

For today
I am reborn
Every part of me
Will never be touched by you
Or someone like you
Ever again

My rebirth today
Has given me hope
Has given me freedom

My Heart No Longer Aches

To feel loved

For I am loved

By those i let love me

My soul no longer craves

To be loved

For I have found love

In myself

I am beautiful

I am amazing

I am a soul to be treasured

Today

I no longer hold onto any part of you

Today

I am reborn

Whole

And at peace

Today I Found Peace

It didn't just happen
But I did
Just notice
Today
I found my peace

I looked deep inside
And instead of feeling
Like I had a cloud
Of doubt
Hanging over my head
I realized
I had stepped into a meadow
Full of life
And colors
I found
Peace

No longer
Am I tormented
By what others think of me

No longer
Do I let their words control me

And my reaction to their words
No longer
Control me
I have found
Peace

I would say I lost a lot of me
And time
But I am me today
Because of all I have lost
And I finally
Found peace
In the pain

I was reminded
I am beautiful
I am amazing
I am unique
I am someone that
If I'm in you're life
You are the lucky one
Because I have chosen you
To share my time with

I have found peace

Home

What is home to me
For it's a place
I've always avoided

Home
Is not a place

For the place
Home
Has no meaning to me

It's never had a chance
For it's always been a place of danger
Insecurity
Unknown
A place I'd rush to leave
And not rush to return

But with you
I see a different life
That could be possible
I see a place

That if you're there
I can't wait to get there
To spend time with you
However much time
This short life will allow

I see a place
I could feel safe
And never be afraid to be me
Act like me
Or talk like me
For with you
I feel
There is no wrong I can do
There is no walking on egg shells

I see a man
I'm not afraid of
I see a man
I can talk to
I see a man
That for the first time
Ever
Has made me feel safe

A word I had long given up on
Ever knowing the meaning of

For fear
Of every one
Every action
Every word
Has been my existence for so long
And safe
Is a foreign feeling
One I'm scared to get used to

For one day
You might walk away
And then I'm left
Living in the biggest fear
I could ever know
Because safe
Will no longer exist

For with your exit
The walls will return
Impenetrable
So I'm never vulnerable again
'Cause living in fear
Is what I know

So home

Is not a place to me

Home

Is you

Because home

Means you feel safe

Protected

Cherished

Impenetrable forces protect you

And that's

How I feel

When I'm with you

You

Are

Home

Once in a While

Someone comes into your life
They may come in slyly
Or they may come crashing in.
But either way,
They change the course of your life,
Forever.

Where once you tolerated not existing.
Just going through the motions
Because you've convinced yourself
This is what you deserve
Can no longer be tolerated.
There is no going back
To feeling nothing again or
To mean nothing to anyone
Once your soul has woken up.

You came in
Both ways
At first.
A glance here and there.
A word exchanged once in a while.

It took one day

For you to break my walls.

One day, for my soul to be zapped alive.

Just one day with you

That was all it took.

Do you know how long I had the walls up?

Do you know how lonely my life was?

Now I'm trying not to fall.

For you have come crashing in.

You have woken my soul.

Window to My Soul

As a child
I was care-free
Impulsive
Unfiltered

As a young adult
Without realizing it
I lost those things
I was calculating
I was sheltered
I was controlled

You came in like a hurricane
Blew my windows wide open
And now
I see a soul
My soul
In all its scars
Its beauty
And its layers

Part of me wants to close that window
For the feelings I felt
Were surreal

I was living

One of my dreams

For real

But the chaos

That is left in your wake

Has me conflicted

I was real with you

And now I'm raw

The window to my soul

Has never been so open

Or so vulnerable

Do I step back

close one side

To make sure I don't get hurt

To make sure my light isn't dimmed

By another careless act

Of my trust?

Or do I leave it wide open

Take all the pain and happiness

That would come

If I just left it open

To take in anything

Life wants to throw at me?

The pain makes me stronger
More resilient
The happiness makes me shine
Bright enough
The lost souls find me
And reach for me
From their dark caverns

The window
To my soul
Is open now

Be careful with it
And if I shut it
Know it's because
The light
Is no longer shining
For you

Phoenix Noel

Calling Karma!

Calling Karma!
For anger has left my soul
and replaced it as a whisper of a candle
that still comes and goes.
But at least the inner rage has gone.
I sleep peacefully now
not tossing and turning.

THEY, don't consume my thoughts anymore.
 I don't stare at the ceiling
planning their ultimate demise
which I'm ashamed now to admit
sometimes made me feel giddy inside.

I relish the idea that Karma will find THEM,
vulnerable, pitiful even.
Oh, sweet revenge how they too will hurt someday!
THEIR emotions will drown in this heavy weighted pain.
My heart races, my fists clench tighter
as I try to squeeze the pain away.
I decide it's not good for me alone
to hold on to this kind of emotional darkness.

What Karma?
No, you didn't get the wrong person.
Frustrating isn't it?
They ignore your siren's call
because THEY believe they have not done wrong.
I bet THEY are sleeping like a baby,
not tossing and turning.
Not even plotting my untimely demise.

I open my eyes.
I scream out loud for Karma to hear.
Enough! THEY have stolen enough of ME
And now it's time to let THEM go!

Karma, what's this that I am feeling?
My breathing is calm.
No more dark images dance in my head.
My body feels lighter.
My fists are unclenched.

Angry images are slowly being replaced
with warm thoughts for those in my life
who have shown me the path
to peace and self-love.
Who taught me an unfathomable lesson

that none of us are leaving here

without emotional scars

but it's up to me to stay in the dark

or find forgiveness and grace.

So long Karma!

I don't need you anymore.

Art and Stones

I am not sure that I want to say that I am grateful
for the lessons life offered.
I have experienced insurmountable emotional pain—
the sudden loss of my brother
betrayal, thus the end of a long love affair
the passing of my beloved father
tragically happening in the blink of an eye
—but it did awaken the writer in me.

I felt like I swallowed a raging inferno!
For there was so much adrenaline inside of me
because with each loss there was another
without the gift of time to process my pain.
In the beginning I chose wine
and yes, carbs too
to deal with this unfamiliar emotional roller coaster from hell.
All that did was make me feel heavier with no energy
or motivation to do better.
So, I released my thoughts on paper
feelings that I was ashamed to admit.
With only one rule to follow:
no self judgment.

I'm just exploring

after all, it began with dear diary

and evolved into something more.

To help release the negative energy

I threw stones into the bay

the heavier the stone the better

while cursing loudly into the wind

trying to make the biggest splash .

But my emotions mocked me

and remained stubbornly inside.

Luckily, I discovered that words come easily to me

and once I released the tap, so to speak

I find that I can't type fast enough

to keep up with my thoughts and emotions.

Writing short stories or poems

has been my saving grace .

I take great pride when I have created.

Yet, I am both excited and fearful

at the thought of my daughters

reading my innermost private thoughts

but maybe they will learn about who I was

when my story is done.

Aside from role as a mother
I want to teach them that
they will learn how to get back up
when life brings them to their knees.
They will see that many women before them
have been on a similar path
and have gotten stronger because of it.
Life is a beautiful mess and they, too, are learning.
I just hope they find their creative outlet
whether it's putting thoughts to paper
or throwing stones into the water
and cursing into the wind
or something else that helps
release their pain and frustration.
I just hope they don't always choose wine
...but never feel guilty about carbs!

Enough!

I know that you are still here
And that despite all my anger
and venomous accusations
cast your way
YOU are still here!

Not that I want you to be
—at least, I don't think so.
No, I want you buried underground
or stuck on a ship
with a one-way pass.
For the pain that you injected into my soul
is too much to bear sometimes.

Forget that simple cliché
because so far time doesn't heal
or help lighten
the weight on my heart.
I feel more protected
and more fearful
to ever love again.

If I'm being honest
the real fear is the unanswered question
that no amount of chocolate or wine can silence:
WHY WASN'T I ENOUGH?

Somewhere during our time
I chose to spend my energy
trying to convince you
that I was enough,
rather than sitting back
and letting you prove
that you were enough for ME!

Now on those days that I falter
—and I will, for I am human after all—
I promise to pull out an old photograph from my youth
look into the eyes of my beautiful
and carefree younger soul
and remember
that I am where I should be right now
and that is ENOUGH!

Grounded

What you did
I haven't forgotten!
But I can hold my head high
when I choose to meet you for coffee
to hear you apologize for the thousandth time
to see your lips move
as you weave excuses.
I don't hear your voice anymore;
I now hear mine.

What you did
I haven't forgotten!

But I'm grounded now.
I know who I am again!
I can look you in the eye
even after love's harsh lesson.
I found my inner strength
that somehow got lost along the way
and that will never be forgotten!

Cafe and Lattes

Living alone has not been easy.

I miss waking up to hearing chatter in the house
the aroma of freshly brewed coffee awakening my senses
giving me an excuse to abandon my cozy bed
and join the commotion in the kitchen.
Plates clattering and rushed voices
kisses on foreheads
as everyone departs for their day.

Now the fresh scent of morning coffee is gone.
The house silent with no other voices and
I could lay in bed as long as I want
for no one is coming.

I begrudgingly walk towards the kitchen.
where I am met with silence
and the dishes where I left them
reminding me that I am alone.

I challenge myself to leave my empty nest.
to go to a place where the coffee fills my senses

with plates rattling and rushed voices
and kisses shared between loved ones.

So, I enter the quaint neighborhood cafe
and feel like I'm home.

Unstuck

I feel stuck behind my desk, trapped inside.
How I long for the future to feel so bright
that anything could happen.
Now I'm here
not where I thought I would be.
How do I get unstuck?

A- job -is -a -job- is- a -job -is- a -job.
It pays the bills but at what cost?
I'm exhausted at the end of the day.
This is not where I thought I would be.
How do I get unstuck?

I come home to an empty house
where once there was a family.
Now it's me and my furry friend
who luckily loves me unconditionally
but this is not where I thought I would be.
How do I get unstuck?

Rinse and repeat!
Why does it have to also be my life?

I do feel grateful for many things:
food on the table
great friends and family
good health
and of course good wine
but this is not where I thought I would be.
I have to get unstuck.

I tell Alexa to play my favorite playlist
the one that I reserve for exercise or long walks
and I find myself getting energy
as I pull out pots and pans
and chop up onions and garlic
to recreate a recipe from my childhood
and now I am dancing in my kitchen!

So, on the days where I feel
like life didn't turn out
the way that I thought it would
I will remember
it's the simple things.

And that it's up to me to get unstuck!

Short Stories

Phoenix Noel

A Moment in Time

The grey skies looming over Tacoma are finally less ominous as I look outside my front window. I am relieved that I can see faint rays of sunlight poking through the clouds. Trying not to tempt fate, I grab the leash off the coatrack, slip it on my dog Rosie, and head out the door. Unfortunately, my coat is snugger than I remember, and I struggle a bit with the zipper. With a heavy sigh, I face the truth that this past winter was spent less on "self-improvement" and more about eating my feelings. Despite this recent epiphany, it is time for our walk because Rosie is beyond excited to leave the confines of our new place. I grab my favorite scarf and ear pods, close the door behind me, and walk down the stairs that lead to the outside. When I step onto the front walk, I pop in my ear pods and resume the podcast about true crime to help keep me focused and alert, while at the same time, work on getting my steps in.

As I walk, I am amused at the thought of how a small dog

can have such strength and determination as I get pulled towards the neighborhood park. I realize that it has been years since I visited a park and I can recall the hours spent chatting with a fellow mom on a bench, while our children played nearby. My regret is that I wish I had said, "Yes," to playing at the park more than, "Sorry, not today." Especially since my children left the proverbial nest. Now it's just me and my furry, yet sometimes judgmental companion accompanying me. As the thought enters my mind, Rosie looks back at me, as if to say, "Come on, human slow poke!"

Picking up my pace, I find myself hoping that we will have the park to ourselves because recently I have been feeling antisocial and don't feel like running into anyone and feel like I need to put on a brave face. Unfortunately, as we reach the park, a male figure is leaning against the old metal swing set.

We are not alone.

Luckily, I am hidden from view, thanks in part to the trees and bushes planted nearby and Rosie hasn't picked up on this stranger's scent. Otherwise, if she does, she will growl or bark loudly and pull on the leash even harder. Interestingly, prior to my breakup she was a very calm dog, but her behavior since then makes me wonder if she is jaded towards all men, or just the ones that remind her of my ex.

Note to future self: If your dog doesn't trust him, then neither should you!

As I approach the curve in the path, I see a pair of old brown loafers disappearing then reappearing behind the bushes. I blame the lack of mental clarity on not enough sleep and polishing off last night's bottle of wine, because it took my brain a minute or two to realize what I am seeing. No, this is not an unusual phenomenon, this is just somebody swinging on the old swing set!

Despite the whispering of dark tales into my ears, I cautiously walk closer to find out who is attached to the brown loafers, only to discover my elderly neighbor Mr. Wylie. I am both surprised and amused that it is him. The week that I moved in, he introduced himself in an odd way, first to Rosie, then to me, giving me reassurance that he is a fellow dog lover. Now, he is here pumping his legs back and forth, but out of sync enough that it looks like he is running through invisible air and wearing the biggest grin on his face!

I can't help but laugh but as I do so, Mr. Wylie's legs abruptly stop moving as he looks over at me. I feel embarrassed wondering if he thinks that I am spying on him. Rather than acting irritated he continues to smile and gesture with his hand for me to come over and join him.

Of course, I want to be neighborly but not sure I want to try to squish my hips into the swing set. Yet, something inside urges me on and I swear I feel a gentle nudge as my feet move towards him. The swing is vacant next to him, and I can't help but feel a little excited as I remember how much I loved to do this when I was a child. Despite my insecurity, I sit down on the swing and feel relieved that I am not as squished as I feared. He looks at me with a weathered grin and eyes that still have a sparkle to them, and I feel my shoulders begin to relax.

I am about to exchange my usual pleasantries but just before I do, I get the sense that if we speak, crazy or not, it will somehow break this childlike spell. Instead, he motions with his hand for my legs to move as he starts to pump his own legs. I do as he silently instructed, now both of us are swinging in sync. It only takes a few minutes until we both lean our heads back and let the feelings of excitement wash over us. Without warning, I release a loud guttural noise and with that some of my emotional pain leaves my body. As if on cue, I hear a similar but more primal noise coming from Mr. Wylie. Together we swing even faster, closing our eyes tightly, tears streaming down our cheeks and our hair dancing wildly in the wind. With each pump, we release the pain from our sudden losses and feel the sadness float away.

When I open my eyes, I somehow actually feel lighter, not in a physical sense, because my coat is still quite snug, but rather an emotional weight has been lifted. When I stop the swing, I make a mental commitment to myself to move on from the aftermath of my breakup, and yes, to cut back on wine. Because, today, spending time at the park helped me realize that I want to appreciate the simple things that bring joy to my life.

I look over at Mr. Wylie and can almost picture what he must have looked like as a young boy. I make a silent promise that I will make more of an effort when I run into him and invite him over for coffee. I want to believe that he and I shared a special moment in time and understand that this moment was a gift, so without saying a word, I smile back, and we spend the next few moments lost in our memories.

Sheila Mengert

Transgender:
Skating on the Edge

I discovered the joys of ice-skating later in life than I could have wished, even though a skating rink existed just across the lake from the home where I spent my high school years. I think I was put off at first by the words, "Figure Skating." In my mind it had something to do with showing off one's figure in the cute little outfits that figure skaters wore. For a young trans-kid, anxious above all else to hide and finally to overcome any aspirations that I entertained of a transgender nature, the idea of wearing figure skates was simply too close to home and a dead giveaway of my true feelings. Even to be part of a skating pair by attempting to hoist and throw a partner into the air was to subject oneself to teasing, if not to outright ostracism, if it ever got out at school. Athleticism was irrelevant if it was accompanied by graceful motions of the arms accompanied by music. Ice-skating, unless it was hockey, was still a sissy sport and that word brought up countless instances of bullying even when doing one's best to avoid any association with anything remotely girly.

For the above reasons it was not until my twenties that I finally embraced figure skating as a welcome vehicle for gender exploration and found an awakening sense of joy in the flow of my body over ice. Of course I immediately carried this new hobby into the rest of my life by requesting that my hair be cut in the wedge-cut made famous by Dorothy Hamil when she captured the hearts of America at the 1976 Winter Olympics in Innsbruck, Austria. I was working in an industrial setting at the time and I no doubt raised a few eyebrows by my unusual projection of a cross-gendered hairstyle combined with all of the other tell-tale signs of early gender experimentation, such as residual nail-polish around the cuticles and a ruby-red tinge of lip-color absorbed ineradicably into the flesh like water in an exceptionally dry desert. The early coming-out stories of trans-people often contain elements of oblivious risk-taking, so welcome it is to finally start expressing what have been hidden feelings throughout youth. The important part of these somewhat embarrassing revelations is to point out the degree of resistance that once met early transition compared to the more charted and sometimes acceptable or even encouraged pathways to divergent gender-expression allowed today.

Recreation might be broken down into segments,

re-creation, for that is precisely what transgender individuals are doing when they come out, first to themselves and only very gradually to other people. The patrolled areas of gender expression are only really evident when one is tempted to cross them. This crossing that seems so odd and unnecessary to others is for transgender people like escaping from North Korea. At first it is exhilarating precisely because it is new. The many years of alienation and fear drop away and suddenly one is skating smoothly over a glistening surface to the sound of Abba and the song "Dancing Queen." The words of various songs sometimes have a personal meaning. The long and dusty corridors of a lonely and frustrated childhood admit light for the first time and one begins to realize that she or he or neither has been living in a haunted house year after year and calling it destiny. The penalties once exacted from trans-persons for cross-gender behaviors were not merely draconian; they were brutal. It takes incredible pressure to risk encountering them, but I felt myself doing so each time I took a step further into the beckoning world that I never knew existed until I crossed its threshold.

Now so many years later I wonder if all that I went through then was really necessary, because I paid a great price then and still am. As the resistance against transgender people places us on a par with illegal immigration, the threat of Communist China, and of a one-world government as issues that cause panic across great swaths of America I can see that we have not yet completely reached a land of safety and equality. At times of discouragement, precisely those times when recreation is most necessary, I think of the days when ice-skating was everything to me. I recall when a county-operated skating rink would only allow me to skate when no public session was going on, perhaps to protect me from the threats that I was occasionally subjected to or to spare the public from having to share the ice with a transgender individual. As an accommodation reminiscent of the treatment once afforded to those with a contagious disease, it at least gave me access to the ice. It all seems so absurd now, but such treatment was once standard operating procedure for people not yet recognized as a discrete and insular minority with equal rights to access to public facilities.

How much more pleasant it is to recall the time that the entire lake froze over and for several days it was safe to skate on, even at night, when no thaw or swimming water-fowl had left hazards to make such natural skating unsafe. It was my last day home for Christmas before returning to my job in the mid-west. I walked out on the dock where throughout my childhood I swam and water-skied. Now that same water was a black sheet of perfectly smooth ice, open in any direction without obstacles or restrictions. I was able to attain any speed or turn about suddenly to skate in backwards cross-overs and to see the white marks in the virgin ice left by my skates in the dim glow from the homes reflected from the surface of the water. I closed my eyes, I recall, and felt only the centripetal forces of speed and turning as I claimed the ice for my own. The sound of my skates was like the sounds of sharpened blades, deep incisions to release past pain and to celebrate freedom.

It was a special occasion and a special time, one now long past and followed by epic eras of LGBT experiences: the advent of AIDS, the struggles for civil rights, and the incomplete recognition of the particular human differences manifested by our communities.

I realize that I have been skating along an edge of a frozen world for most of my life, twirling about in circles, and sometimes breaking free into open-water where I could forge new paths and see the record of my life behind me as on that night, now so long ago, when the white streaks left behind by my skates revealed that I was there.

Elizabeth Wong

Perfect

Miri held up the blue cotton fabric up to the doll's body. It had white flowers all over the blue background, and it reminded her of some far off memory long ago, viewed through a CRT TV. The print wasn't very large, nor was the fabric itself; only a fat quarter after all. The doll was on the larger side, about two feet tall, but she was certain she could still make something substantial out of it. It's brown glass eyes stare at her, smiling at her with the slightly crooked soft smile that she painted on herself.

She recalled the day the doll's head arrived in the mail. It had been an expensive purchase for just a doll head, but after weeks of hesitation, Miri had finally justified the indulgence during a particularly rough week. The head had come in a black wooden box, cushioned by soft satin pillows, its blank face offering no hint of its future expression beyond the hollows of its eyes and nose. Holding the smooth, cool resin, Miri felt a connection far removed from the vinyl and rubbery toys of her childhood, or even the porcelain dolls she'd seen in antique shops.

The fabric she now considered was unlike anything she'd used for doll clothing before. Contemplating its use, she debated over creating another skirt but dismissed the idea in favor of a more challenging project. She feared wasting the material on an unsuccessful endeavor but also recognized the futility of crafting something uninspired.

Setting the doll in a sitting position, Miri examined its painted face, her gaze lingering on a tiny smudge above its eyebrow. Despite numerous repaintings, she remained critical of her work, a trait she wondered if was innate or instilled by her perfection-demanding parents. Falling short of perfection always meant harsh punishment. Shaking off the thought, she focused on the doll's body, which she had painstakingly selected to match her vision of elegance and realism, despite its cost. It had taken a while to find a body she liked and even longer for it to arrive.

Searching through her pattern box, she found a design for a long-sleeved, floor-length dress, reminiscent of the elegant attire worn by one of Miri's neighbors. She had always admired such dresses but felt constrained by her own physique. Yet, through her doll, she could explore these fashions, the doll a perfect blank canvas for the clothes she couldn't wear herself, the clothes small enough Miri could afford to make them.

She chose a dark red cotton for the dress, a fabric too expensive for her own wardrobe but perfect for the doll. After tracing and cutting the pattern, Miri quickly assembled the dress with her sewing machine, adding snap buttons for a final touch. The result was a stunning red dress that complemented the doll's slender form. Just beautiful.

Inspired, Miri decided to create a bolero jacket from the blue fabric, envisioning how it would enhance the dress. *Ah, you'll look so wonderful,* she thought, *even though you look wonderful in anything.* As she worked, Miri's mind drifted and she remembered being forced to wear all sorts of uncomfortable things because her mother insisted, how she had to always behave perfectly or face her family's wrath. There were times when she felt like a doll, made to be perfect, just a thing others could squeeze every drop of worth from, until Miri was left broken. Anytime she tried to do something for her self, something unique and creative, her parents would dismiss it, preferring her to do the same things as the children of their friends and neighbors. She tried changing every bit of who she was so they could be proud of her—and they were, sometimes—but each achievement only brought more and more demands. *Throw away those childish things. Ignore those thoughts—they're not relevant to your goals. Why are you always so angry? Why are you so sad? You should be thankful for what you've been given.* Miri shook her head. Foul memories, indeed. She turned back to the task at hand.

Determined to provide the doll with freedom she never had, she designed the bolero to allow easy movement. The finished bolero, paired with the dress, was a testament to her skill and vision, imperfect yet deeply satisfying. Holding the doll, Miri felt a rare moment of contentment and pride.

Biographies

Michelle Lee

Michelle Lee is a Pacific Northwest native with an imagination open to possibilities. In her downtime, Michelle is an avid reader, loves to explore different areas in the northwest, speaks fluent sarcasm, and enjoys spending time with her significant other and their two cats. She loves to hear from readers and can be found on Facebook and Instagram.

Dakoda Foxx

Dakoda Foxx is a writer, actor, artist, and paralegal. She is dedicated to making a positive impact on the people she comes in contact with. She advocates for people's rights and dedicates her life to help make a change for others. She hopes her readers see that there is light at the end of any tunnel, in any situation. Dakoda's memoir, *The Magic in the Nightmare that was Me*, is a story of survival, perserverance, and a spirit that refused to be broken. She has also written a pocket-sized book in the *Haunting of Orchard House* series called *Paranoia*. Dakoda books are available at www.BlueForgePress.com. Find her on Facebook at: https://www.facebook.com/DakodaFoxxAuthorPage

Jennifer DiMarco

Winner of Bumbershoot and PNWC poetry awards, Seattle Times bestselling novelist Jennifer DiMarco first toured nationally as an author when she was nineteen years old having written novels since the age of ten. The first sixteen years of her career included the publication of contemporary drama, high fantasy, science fiction, poetry, and mystery novels as well as the production of two short films and three stage plays. During a twenty-year hiatus from prose, DiMarco married, raised two children, and worked as a filmmaker writing and directing more than a dozen feature films, half a dozen mini series, and more than a hundred short films, before returning to prose with "*Hannah at Night*" in 2020. DiMarco lives in the Pacific Northwest with her wife, author and actor Brianne, and their adult children, author and illustrator Maxwell, and actor and illustrator Faith. Find all of Jennifer's work at www.BlueForgePress.com

Bree Indigo

Bree Indigo is a poet and songwriter. She was previously published in the three previous volumes of *Rise* (*Reflection, Resurrection,* and *Revolution*), and the first five volumes of the horror anthology *Unnerving* (*Monstrosity, Descent, Eclipse, Wicked* and *Nightfall*), all available at www.BlueForgePress.com. Her first memoir, *Unreliable Narrator*, is forthcoming by Blue Forge Press. Indigo lives with her wife and their children in the Pacific Northwest. Find her on Instagram @bree_indigo

Jonielle McMurtrey

Jonielle McMurtrey has been writing poetry since high school. She has found writing poems as a way to connect with various souls throughout her life. She now lives in a small town in northern Arizona, after living most her life in the great northwest. Moving to Arizona was where Jonielle found much healing and self expression through the suns rays and she hopes the sun can radiate off her to brighten others lives as it has brightened hers.

Phoenix Noel

"Oops I Did it Again..." should be the name of Phoenix Noel's autobiography, because she finds herself starting over at age... well, let's just say it's the new 30! The ending of a nine year relationship that awoke her creative side, urging her to express her anguish with words rather than a sledge hammer. While packing boxes and moving her two human daughters and her fur-baby to a new home in the Seattle area, Phoenix took up a pencil and began to write. To her surprise, she found that her feelings of betrayal and anger turned into poems and short stories that inspired her and awoke her inner fire. If you are looking for something a little sassy and a little dark, with a touch of naughty, look for more stories coming soon and write to Phoenix at phoenixnoel302@gmail.com

Sheila Mengert

Sheila Mengert is a transwoman and writer advocating for social change through systems thinking and organization design. Sheila sees history as the bondage of youth to the outdated aspirations of prior social models characterized by age-based inequality where youth is colonized to create scarcity of resources and to relieve the dying generations of anxiety at their own waning powers and vanishing dreams. If an apocalyptic style of thinking and current crises can yield to a critical reassessment then a transfer of influence, values, and assumptions can empower youth to use interconnected and cooperative populations as ecosystems to spread enlightened goals in a post-empire and post-colonial world.

Elizabeth Wong

Elizabeth Wong has been wanting to tell her stories for years, and now they are finally coming out of her headspace and into reality. When they are not written out, they are drawn out by her in the form of graphic novels. Other interests of hers are taking walks, photography, making games, and robotics.